ANN ARBOR DISTRICT LIBRARY

31621012037483

S0-AHJ-864

J
468
Ro

Diego Wants To Be

Diego Quiere Ser

Written and illustrated by Doris Rodríguez
Escrito e ilustrado por Doris Rodríguez

Highsmith
PRESS

Fort Atkinson, Wisconsin

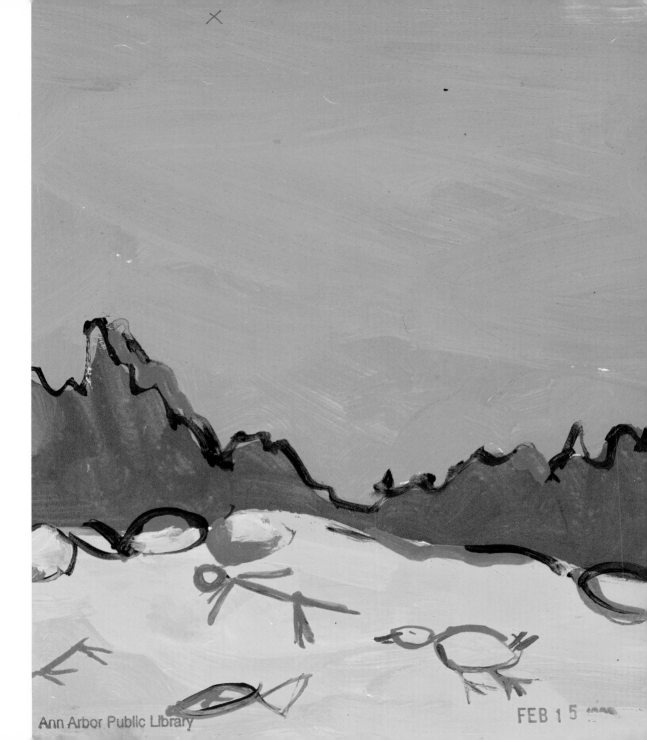

Ann Arbor Public Library

FEB 1 5

Published by Highsmith Press
W5527 Highway 106
P.O. Box 800
Fort Atkinson, Wisconsin 53538-0800
800-558-2110

Copyright ©1994 by Doris Rodríguez

Author photo: Rodolfo Mari
The author wishes to acknowledge that she has drawn her inspiration and
portions of her text from *El Niño,* written by M. Benitez Carrasco, music
composed by Ruben Fuentes. *El Niño* is copyrighted © 1981 by CEFUMA, and all
rights are reserved. Permission to use the text for this book was
granted by Ruben Fuentes, CEFUMA.

All rights reserved. Printed in Canada.
Except as permitted under the United States Copyright Act of 1976, no part
of this publication may be reproduced or distributed in any form or by any means,
or stored in a data base or retrieval system, without the prior written permission of
the publisher.

The paper used in this publication meets the minimum requirements of American
National Standard for Information Science - Permanence of Paper for Printed
Library Material. ANSI/NISO Z39.48-1992

Library of Congress Cataloging-in-Publication Data

    Rodríguez, Doris, 1967–
        Diego wants to be / written and illustrated by Doris Rodríguez =
    Diego quiere ser / escrito e ilustrado por Doris Rodríguez.
          p.   cm.
        Summary: Diego can't wait to grow up and imagines being a fish, a
    bird, and a dog instead of a little boy, but as an old man he has a different
    point of view.
        ISBN 0-917846-35-4 : $15.00
        [1. Animals--Fiction. 2. Growth--Fiction. 3. Spanish language
    materials--Bilingual.] I. Title. II. Title: Diego quiere ser.
    PZ73.R6285 1994   94-3024

ISBN 0-917846-35-4

To Brooke Goffstein,
David Allender and Juan Acosta.

Diego estaba triste
porque no le gustaba
ser niño.

Diego was sad
because he did not like
being a child.

Se fué al rio porque deseaba
ser pez. Metió sus pies al agua
pero estaba tan fría ...

He went to the river because
he wanted to be a fish. He put
his feet into the water, but it
was so cold ...

... que tiritó y ya no quiso ser pez.

... that he shivered and did not want to be a fish anymore.

Miró al cielo y
quiso ser ave.

He looked up into
the sky and wanted
to be a bird.

Trepó por el árbol más alto,
pero estaba tan alto que ya no
quiso ser ave.

He climbed up the tallest tree,
but it was so tall that he did
not want to be a bird anymore.

Diego quería ser
perro.

Diego wanted to be
a dog.

Comenzó a ladrarle
a un gato,

He started barking
at a cat,

pero ladró tanto hasta
cansarse. Y ya no quiso
ser perro.

---

but he barked so much that his
voice got tired. And he did not
want to be a dog anymore.

Diego no quiso ser niño,

Diego did not want to be a
child,

ni pez,

nor a fish,

ni ave,

nor a bird,

ni perro.

---

nor a dog.

Quería ser hombre,

He wanted to be a
man,

y comenzó a crecer.

and he started to
grow up.

Cuando envejeció,

When he became an old man,

pensó en volver a
ser niño otra vez,
pero su madurez le
hizo comprender
que ...

he thought about
being a child again,
but he was wise
enough to know ...

3 1621 00647 0401

... era demasiado
tarde.

... that it was too
late.

About the Author and Illustrator

Doris Rodríguez is a native of the Dominican Republic. She studied architecture at the Pontifica Universidad Católica Madre y Maestra, and graduated Magna Cum Laude from the Alto de Chavon School of Design. She has taught painting and drawing, and gained additional experience as a newspaper illustrator and assistant art director in an advertising firm. Currently, she is completing her studies at the Parsons School of Design in New York City. Her work has been exhibited in the Dominican Republic and the United States.

She uses bold Caribbean colors, strong images, and sun-drenched settings that are drawn from her childhood to complement this powerful but simple story. Her illustrations were painted in acrylic on paper. Music is another of her major interests, and it served as the inspiration for *Diego Wants To Be*.

Photo by Rodolfo Mari

About the Multicultural Publishers Exchange Children's Book Award

The Multicultural Publishers Exchange (MPE) was established to foster greater awareness of the rich diversity of resources available from independent publishers devoted to African, Hispanic, Asian and Native American authors, illustrators, and subjects. Because only a limited number of children's books by authors and illustrators of these cultures have been published, MPE and Highsmith Press jointly sponsored a national competition in 1993 to encourage previously unpublished authors and illustrators. *Diego Wants To Be* was selected to receive this award by a jury drawn from the MPE's membership.

MPE was reorganized in 1994 as the Multicultural Publishing and Education Council (MPEC). A description of their programs and their address can be located in the most recent edition of the Guide to Multicultural Resources (Biennial, Highsmith Press).

OUTREACH

MAR : 1995